FRANKIE'S MAGIC FOOTBALL

FRANKIE'S KANGAROO CAPER

FRANK LAMPARD

LITTLE, BROWN BOOKS FOR YOUNG READERS
www.lbkids.co.uk

LITTLE, BROWN BOOKS FOR YOUNG READERS

First published in Great Britain in 2015 by
Little, Brown Books for Young Readers

3 5 7 9 10 8 6 4 2

A CIP catalogue record for this book
is available from the British Library.

ISBN 978-0-349-12451-3

Typeset in Cantarell by M Rules
Printed and bound in Great Britain by
Clays Ltd, St Ives plc

Papers used by LBYR are from well-managed forests
and other responsible sources.

MIX
Paper from
responsible sources
FSC® C104740

Little, Brown Books for Young Readers,
an imprint of Hachette Children's Group and
published by Hodder and Stoughton Limited
338 Euston Road, London NW1 3BH

An Hachette UK Company
www.hachette.co.uk

www.lbkids.co.uk

*To my mum Pat, who encouraged
me to do my homework in between
kicking a ball all around the house,
and is still with me every step
of the way.*

Welcome to a fantastic Fantasy League – the greatest football competition ever held in this world or any other!

You'll need four on a team, so choose carefully. This is a lot more serious than a game in the park. You'll never know who your next opponents will be, or where you'll face them.

So lace up your boots, players, and good luck! The whistle's about to blow!

The Ref

CHAPTER 1

A few specks of rain spattered against the car window. Outside, the sky was slate grey, even though it was supposed to be summer. *Typical English weather*, thought Frankie. It was the last day of the half-term holidays. Normally, he'd have been out playing football,

but his mum and dad had offered
to take them all to the safari park
instead. So far they'd seen African
mammals, the reptile house,
penguins and sea lions, and a
massive gorilla.

Frankie read the sign as they
waited in the queue of cars outside
the monkey enclosure.

Please close all windows and doors.
Please do not feed the animals.
Please do not beep your horns –
the monkeys don't like it!

"I hope they don't jump on my
car!" said Frankie's dad, who was

4

in the driving seat. "I've just had it washed."

Frankie peered out of the window as they drove in. He couldn't see a single animal. Where were they all hiding?

"What's your favourite creature in the safari park so far, Frankie?" asked Louise. She and Charlie were sitting in the back with Frankie. Max, Frankie's dog, sat in the rear of the car, peering out of the back window.

"I like the cheetahs!" said Frankie. "The guide book said they were the fastest creatures on legs. Imagine being able to run at seventy miles an hour. No defender could catch you!"

"The cheetahs looked pretty lazy to me," said his dad. "They were just lounging around today."

"Like you on the sofa when the football's on, Dad," said Frankie.

Everyone laughed.

"I loved the sea lions," said Louise. "They're so clever!"

Frankie agreed. They'd watched a display in the sea lion tank, as the animals leapt out of the water, jumping through hoops while their keepers tossed them fish. One had even splashed Frankie's dad with its tail.

"They were pretty good at football
too," said Frankie's mum. "One
could balance a ball on its nose!"

"The orang-utan was best," said
Charlie.

"Why?" said Louise."Because he
had red hair like you?"

"No," said Charlie, grinning.

"Because of his reach, of course.
He'd make an amazing goalkeeper.
Hey — look at that!" He pointed with
his goalie glove out of his window,
and Frankie saw a black shape
running along a branch.

"It's a monkey!" said Louise.

Frankie steadied his camera as
more monkeys appeared through
the leaves. One was watching their
car and eating a piece of mushy
fruit. Frankie waved to catch its
attention. "Say cheese!" he called.
The monkey swung down from the
tree, then leapt out of sight over
the top of the car before Frankie
could get a picture.

"Where'd he go?" asked Louise, looking around.

Thump!

Something hit the roof of the car.

"Oh no," said Frankie's dad, twisting in his seat. "He wants to say hello!"

A small wrinkled face peered over the top of the car, looking into Frankie's window. The monkey's mouth twisted in a smile and it laid a palm against the glass.

"They're so like us, aren't they?" said Louise.

The monkey vanished.

"Thank goodness for that!" said Frankie's dad, continuing to drive slowly. "Now it can go and bother someone else."

Thumpety–thumpety–thump.

Footsteps bounced along the roof, and the monkey landed on the bonnet.

Frankie's dad put on the brakes gently and the car came to a stop. "Oh, marvellous!" he sighed.

The monkey began to fiddle with the windscreen wipers, pulling at one until it twanged back into place.

"Maybe we should call the park rangers," muttered Frankie's dad.

"Don't be silly," said his mum. "It's only playing. And look, the same thing is happening to everyone else!"

Through the front windscreen,

Frankie saw she was right. All the cars had monkeys leaping over them, causing mischief.

Frankie's dad continued to drive slowly.

The monkey hopped on to the wing mirror, then disappeared again. Max whined from the back of the car. Frankie turned and saw the monkey perched on the rear of the car. It seemed to be fiddling with something.

"Lou, you don't think monkeys can open boots, do you?" he said.

Before his friend could answer, there was a soft click, and the boot opened.

"Oh no!" said Frankie's mum. "Better stop the car."

Frankie watched as the monkey looked first at Max, who was baring his teeth, then at something else. Frankie's football bag.

Frankie realised what was inside, and his heart began to beat faster.

"My football . . . " he whispered to Louise.

The monkey reached into the bag and took out the battered football. Then the creature bounced away. Frankie stared at his friends in horror. A monkey had stolen their magic football!

CHAPTER 2

"Thank goodness for that!" said
Frankie's dad, driving off while
looking in the mirror. "I was
worried that animal might steal my
tools!"

"Or our picnic," said Frankie's
mum. She'd packed a wicker basket
full of sausage rolls, cheese and

pickle sandwiches, apples, Frankie's
favourite crisps and bottles of
lemonade. Max was nudging his
nose beneath the lid of the basket,
drool collecting at the corners of
his mouth. Frankie pulled him away
and Max licked Frankie's face.
He seemed to have forgotten all
about the monkey thief. *Nothing's
more important than food*, Frankie
thought. *Not to Max.*

"At least he didn't try to steal
Max!" said Charlie. The dog stopped
licking Frankie and whined.

Frankie stared out of the open
boot. The monkey was standing
in the middle of the road, making

screeching noises while holding the ball above its head as if it were the FA Cup.

"It looks rather pleased with itself," said Frankie's mum.

The monkey dropped the ball on to the ground, then gave it a kick. It rolled a few metres. The monkey made a chattering sound like laughter and kicked it again.

"It's playing football!" said Louise.

The monkey was about to kick the ball again when another monkey shot past and grabbed the ball.

It hurled the football to one of its friends, who scampered quickly up the trunk of a tree. Frankie lost sight of the creature among the leaves, but he could see more monkeys swarming towards the tree.

"Dad, you have to go back!" said Frankie.

"Don't be daft," said his dad. "We need to get out of here before they do any more damage."

"But . . . "

"Your father's right," said Frankie's mum. "You can hardly climb the tree and get it back. We'll buy you a new ball, don't worry. That one *was* rather shabby."

That's not the point, thought Frankie. *That football is special!*

As soon as they'd left the monkey enclosure, Frankie's dad climbed out of the car and shut the boot.

A ranger came over. "Is something the matter, sir?" she asked.

"I'm afraid one of the monkeys managed to open the boot and take my son's football," he said.

The ranger's eyes widened. "Gosh, how clever. Was it a little one?"

"Yes!" said Frankie. "Can you get it back, please?"

The ranger grimaced. "I'm afraid that's Momo. He's quite the mischief-maker. The best place to look is probably the kangaroo enclosure. It joins the side of the monkey section — Momo often throws things over the fence!"

"Thanks," said Frankie. "Let's go!"

"Tell you what," said Frankie's mum. "We'll go after we've had lunch, all right?"

Frankie didn't want to wait, but

he didn't want to reveal the truth about the magic football either. He didn't think his parents or the park rangers would believe that it could open magic portals into the past or other worlds entirely!

"Can we go *now*?" he asked. "I'm not that hungry."

"Me neither," said Louise quickly.

"I am," said Charlie. Louise glared at him. "But I can wait," he added.

"All right," said Frankie's mum. "If you insist. Maybe we can eat in the car."

"Just be careful not to get crumbs on the seats," added Frankie's dad.

Louise put a hand on Frankie's

shoulder. "Don't worry," she said.
"It will be OK."

Frankie wished he could feel as
confident as his friend.

With the magic football loose
in the safari park, *anything* could
happen. What if it transported
a troop of monkeys to Ancient
Rome, or the top of the Eiffel
Tower? Momo might be clever for
a monkey, but Frankie doubted he
could find his way back to the safari
park.

They drove along a track and
soon reached the Australian section
of the park. Frankie absent-
mindedly munched on a sandwich.

Louise was feeding bits of sausage roll to Max.

"Apparently there are emus, koalas, crocodiles and all sorts," said Frankie's mum, reading the guide book.

Frankie was only interested in the kangaroos, but the gate to the kangaroo area was closed when they pulled up. A ranger held up a hand. She was speaking on a radio. Eventually, she came over to the car. Frankie's dad wound down the window. Frankie was worried. *Something's going on . . .*

"Sorry, sir," said the ranger, "but you won't be able to come in. We have a safety issue. A 'foreign object' has found its way into the enclosure and it's sending the kangaroos a bit batty!"

"Oh, really?" said Frankie's mum. "The foreign object wouldn't happen to be my son's football, would it? A monkey stole it."

"It *is* a ball," said the ranger, frowning. "Haven't you read the signs? You shouldn't have been playing with it in the park."

"It was the monkey's fault!" Charlie muttered, from the back seat beside Frankie.

Another car beeped behind them. A queue was forming.

Frankie climbed out of the car.

He scanned the fence, to see if there was a way through.

"If we could just get hold of the football again . . . " he said to Louise.

At that moment, another ranger came through a side gate. He held something that was making a horrible wailing sound. Frankie edged closer and saw a bundle of fur with huge ears and sad, black eyes. It was a baby kangaroo!

"Look what I found, Gill," he said to the ranger talking with Frankie's parents. "It's Madge's joey."

"Funny name for a kangaroo," said Charlie. He was still holding a sandwich in his goalie glove.

The female ranger raised an eyebrow. "A joey is what we call a baby kangaroo," she said. "Normally they spend most of the time in their mother's pouch. Madge must have dropped her by accident."

The ranger cradling the baby kangaroo shrugged. "She's nowhere to be found," he said. "We think she must have jumped the fence."

Frankie gazed up at the fence. It was at least five metres tall. No way could a kangaroo jump over it!

The baby kangaroo gave another terrified call. "Poor thing," said Louise.

"It's trying to call to its mother,"

said the ranger. "We need to find her quickly."

A cold dread crept over Frankie. *What if the football has something to do with this?*

From Charlie and Louise's stares, he guessed they were thinking the same thing. Several other visitors were joining the group, all wanting to get a look at the baby kangaroo and talking over each other. Frankie peered back towards the enclosure, where the ranger had left the gate slightly ajar.

We might not get another chance!

He nudged Louise's arm and gestured towards the gate. She

nodded, and tugged Charlie's shirt. Together with Max, they rushed for the enclosure.

"This feels strictly against the rules," said Louise, as they slipped inside.

"We don't have a choice," said Frankie. "We need to get the football back before it does any more harm!"

It wasn't long before they found the kangaroos. They were gathered in a small circle, and all looked up as Frankie and his friends approached, their ears twitching. Frankie swallowed – up close, they were *big*! Their legs looked like they could deliver a nasty kick.

"There it is!" said Louise. She pointed, and Frankie saw that one of the kangaroos was standing right over the magic football.

"What now?" muttered Charlie. "It doesn't look like it's ready to pass."

Frankie stepped ahead of his friends, moving slowly. "Er . . . hello, nice kangaroo," he said, feeling very silly and very scared.

"I don't think it speaks human," said Louise. "Maybe clap or something – scare it off."

Frankie clapped loudly several times. The kangaroo didn't budge a muscle.

Frankie felt something brush past his ankles. "Max! No!" he cried.

But his dog bravely trotted forward. The kangaroo gave a little hop backwards, scuffing the ground. Then, with a grunt, it kicked the ball hard towards them.

Charlie jumped to save it, but it shot over his head and hit the wire mesh fence with a bright flash.

Frankie blinked and shielded his eyes. When the light died, he saw a familiar circle of swirling light where the ball had hit the fence. The ball rolled back to Charlie, who picked it up. "Thank goodness!" he said. "Let's get back to the car

before your parents notice we're gone."

He started back towards the gate, but Frankie called out to him. "Wait, Charlie, we can't!"

"Why?" said Charlie, turning round.

Frankie pointed at the portal. It was already beginning to shrink. "I've worked out what happened. The missing kangaroo must have gone through a portal made by the ball. We have to follow and get her back!"

As if on cue, they heard the joey's sad cries carrying towards them through the swirling light.

"I guess you're right," said Charlie.

"Let's go, then," said Louise. Frankie picked up Max. "Ready for another adventure?" he asked.

Max barked in reply.

"I think that was a 'yes'," said Frankie.

Without another word, he ran towards the shrinking portal and leapt through.

CHAPTER 3

Frankie found himself standing in a barren desert. He stared around him at dry, red earth littered with a few scrubby plants and bushes. The sun shone down from the blue sky above. His skin prickled under the glare — it was like standing next to the open oven door. He turned full circle, staring at the land that stretched flat all the way to the distant horizon.

No, not completely flat . . .

Rising above the plain several miles away was a wide mountain with a flat top. It shimmered in the heat haze.

"I think I know where we are!" said Louise. "That's Uluru!"

"Pardon?" said Charlie.

"That's the traditional name for it, anyway," said Louise. "Some people call it Ayers Rock. We're in Australia!"

"That makes sense," said Frankie. "We came from the Australian

enclosure, after all. The magic football has transported us halfway around the world!"

"I've always wanted to come to Australia," said Charlie. "But I wanted to try surfing, and there don't seem to be many waves around here."

"There's not much water of any sort," said Louise, fanning her face with a hand. "Uluru is in the outback of the Northern Territory."

"Well, the kangaroo must be around somewhere," said Frankie, but he didn't feel hopeful. This place was vast!

Charlie gave Frankie his

football, and they set off across the dry landscape. They hadn't gone far when the shape of a building became visible ahead. Frankie hoped they'd be able to get some water. His throat was already parched and sweat was dripping down his back. Max's tongue was lolling and Charlie's skin was flushed bright red. He still hadn't taken off his gloves, though.

"Duck!" cried a voice.

Frankie instinctively crouched, but Charlie leapt sideways and snatched something blurring through the air. A girl came running up to them from behind a bush. A small tan-coloured puppy ran at her heels, yapping and jumping up at her waist.

"Good catch!" she said.

Charlie blushed as he stood up. "It's kind of my speciality," he said, turning his gloves back and forth.

Frankie saw that he was holding a carved stick, bent in the middle.

"Ooh, stick!" said Max. The little puppy came out from behind the girl's legs, wagging its tail.

"Shhhh!" Frankie told Max, as his dog opened his mouth to say something else. He didn't want to have to explain a talking pet to this girl.

"It's not a stick, it's a boomerang!" said Louise.

The girl nodded. "I'm just out practising. Where did you come from?" She glanced at Charlie. "And why is he wearing gloves in this heat?"

"I like to be ready!" said Charlie. He handed back the boomerang.

"Ready for what? Winter?" smiled the girl. "It's nearly forty degrees out here."

"We need your help," said Frankie, thinking quickly. "We're . . . tourists." He held up his camera. "We're trying to get a snap of a kangaroo." He thought back to the joey, crying for its mum. *We have to reunite them!*

The girl grinned wider. "Well, you've come to the right place. There are more kangaroos than people in Australia. I'm Alba, by the way. My family live in the Uluru National Park."

"Is there anywhere to go surfing?" asked Charlie, hopefully.

"I'm afraid not," said the girl, giggling. "I've never even seen the sea!"

Frankie introduced himself. "And this is Louise and Charlie, and Max, my dog."

"This is Dingo," said Alba, stroking her little puppy.

"Funny name for a dog," said Max, peering out from behind Frankie's legs.

"Who said that?" asked Alba.

"I did!" said Frankie.

Alba frowned. "Well, he's called Dingo, because he *is* a dingo. His

43

mother must have abandoned him, and a shelter took him in. My family adopted him. Technically, that makes him a wild dog, but he's really friendly."

Dingo licked her hand.

"So," said Frankie, lifting his camera again. "Any chance you can help us find a kangaroo?"

"Sure!" said Alba. "They tend to go to watering holes. All we need to do is find one, and we'll find kangaroos."

"Great!" said Frankie. "Which way?"

"Hold on," said Alba. "First we need to get you guys some sun

cream and hats. You'll fry out
here!" She pointed to the buildings.
"That's my place — let's stop off
before we go on our kangaroo
quest."

CHAPTER 4

"Charlie, you look like a ghost!" said
Louise.

Frankie laughed too. Charlie's
face was completely covered in
white smears of sun cream. "Better
safe than sorry," he said.

"Everyone ready?" asked Frankie.
They were standing on the wooden

veranda of Alba's home while she fetched water bottles from inside. He was wearing a sunhat, just like Charlie. Louise had a parasol. "Now you *really* look like tourists!" said Alba, as she emerged.

A man peered through the window behind her. *He looks about a hundred years old*, Frankie thought.

"That's my granddad," said Alba. "He looks after me because my parents work in the city."

The man nodded, and Frankie waved. He started down the steps. Better to get going quickly, before the old man started asking awkward questions about their parents.

Alba led them away from the house, between the scrubby plants.

Max barked, sniffing at the ground.

"He's found something!" said Frankie, rushing over.

Max was standing over a couple of two-pronged footprints, side by side.

"Are they made by a kangaroo?" he asked.

"Strange!" said Alba, peering at the marks. "They are kangaroo prints, but the weird thing is they appear from nowhere! See — there's no trail. It's almost like it just dropped out of the sky." Alba was right. There were no other marks that led up to the spot.

Frankie glanced at his friends. *If this is the kangaroo that came through the portal, that's exactly what did happen.*

"Let's track it!" he said.

The footprints stretched away in a zigzagging pattern.

"The kangaroo seems pretty confused," said Alba.

"Makes sense," muttered Louise to Frankie. "She's not used to the outback."

The ground was littered with rocks and bushes baked by the sun. Frankie wiped the moisture from his brow. It felt liked he'd played a whole ninety minutes of football already.

Max suddenly leapt in the air, yapping wildly.

"What is it, boy?" asked Frankie, rushing towards him. Charlie grabbed his arm and pulled him back.

"Don't! It's a snake!"

Frankie shuddered as a large black snake with white rings uncoiled from beside a stone, tongue flickering in a low hiss.

"It's a Bandy Bandy snake!" said Alba. "Your dog probably disturbed its midday nap."

"Is it venomous?" asked Louise.

"Oh, yes," said Alba, quite cheerfully. "Not fatal though."

The snake retreated back into the shade of the rock.

From then on, Frankie watched exactly where he put his feet. Soon the ground dipped, and they found themselves following a narrow gorge of red stone. At the bottom it opened out to a pool of crystal clear water.

"Where does the water come from?" Charlie asked.

"From underground," said Alba. "There are deep reserves trapped there for thousands of years, since the last ice age . . . Wait! Look!"

As they rounded a slight bend, Frankie saw a single kangaroo drinking at the water's edge. It was bigger than Frankie had been expecting — about two metres tall — and it had strong-looking legs and a thick tail.

"There's your kangaroo," whispered Alba. "Are you going to take a picture?"

"Er . . . " Frankie didn't know what to say. He realised that finding the kangaroo was only half the problem. Somehow they had to create a portal and get the thing home! He took a couple of shots on his camera, to give him time to think.

"Ruff! Ruff!" barked Dingo, excited to spot the kangaroo.

The kangaroo's head shot up.

"Quiet, Dingo!" said Alba.

But her dog had already set off, right towards the kangaroo.

"Badly trained," muttered Max.

Frankie and the others burst out of their hiding place. The kangaroo turned and bounded away with huge leaps. Dingo followed, yapping wildly.

"Dingo, come back!" Alba called.

"Stop, Madge!" said Frankie.

He sprinted after Madge and Dingo, but the animals were already far ahead. Soon they were just dots, streaking towards the mountain on the horizon. Frankie stopped, panting for breath.

Now we've got two animals to track down!

CHAPTER 5

Alba reached Frankie's side.
"Dingo won't be able to survive
on his own," she said, her voice
cracking and her eyes filling up
with tears. "You have to help me
get him back."

Frankie put his arm around
her shoulder, staring after the

departing animals. "Of course we will," he said.

"You called that kangaroo Madge!" said Alba, sniffing.

"You must have misheard," said Charlie, quickly.

"We won't be able to catch them on foot," said Louise. "They're too fast and it's too far."

Alba nodded. "I know just the thing," she said. "Camels!"

Charlie was huffing and puffing. "Camels? I'm no expert, but I don't think camels live in Australia."

"They don't, normally," said Alba. Frankie was glad to see her mood brightening. "But there's a ranch near here that runs tours to Uluru. I know the two boys who live there — Neil and Kyle. They use camels to take the tourists."

Alba set off back the way they'd come, and Frankie followed with his friends. This was turning into quite a trek! On the way, Alba threw her boomerang. It whizzed through the air, then curved in a graceful arc and spun back towards them. Each time she caught it neatly. Frankie watched, fascinated at her skills.

"You're good at that!" said Charlie.

Alba grinned. "My grandfather taught me."

"Can I have a go?" said Frankie.

Alba handed him the boomerang, and showed him how to grip it properly. Frankie pulled back his arm and hurled it into the sky. It landed on the dusty ground about thirty metres away.

"Oh," said Frankie. "Why didn't it come back?"

"You just need a bit of practise," said Alba.

Soon they reached a group of low huts made of wood. Inside a fenced-off area a herd of camels were munching on hay.

"Hello!" called Alba. "Anyone home?"

Two boys came out of one of the shacks, both four or five years older than them. "Hi Alba," said the elder of the two, while his younger brother sat on a fence. "What can we do for you?"

"We need to ride out to Uluru," said Alba.

The boy shook his head. "We can't help — my parents are leading a group out there now."

Frankie stepped forward. "Can't we borrow some camels?" he asked.

The boy shrugged, then pointed at Alba's boomerang. "You give us that, and we'll saddle up a couple of camels."

Alba looked unsure. "But . . . my grandpa gave me this! I can't . . . "

"Guess you don't want to get to Uluru that bad," said Kyle.

The younger boy jumped down from the fence. "How about that football, then?" he said, pointing at the round shape in Frankie's hands.

Alba looked at Frankie hopefully. "Give it to him," she said. "Come on — it looks about a hundred years old anyway."

Frankie hesitated. He couldn't give them the football — it was their only way home! But Alba was so upset without her dingo and he needed to get the kangaroo back to its baby. What could he do?

"Tell you what," said Louise, interrupting his thoughts. "We'll give you the football *and* the boomerang . . ."

Alba gasped, "No, you can't!"

" . . . if you can beat us at a game of football," Louise finished.

Great idea, Lou! thought Frankie. It was risky, but it was the only choice they had.

Kyle looked at his younger brother Neil and winked. "You're on."

Alba rushed up to Louise and Frankie. "What have you done? They'll easily beat you!"

"No, they won't," said Frankie, feeling determined. *We can't afford to lose.*

"Two on two," he said to the ranch kids. "The goal is between the two gate-posts at either end of the yard. First goal wins."

"Let's do this," said Kyle. "Alba —
you throw the ball in, and no
cheating."

"I hope you know what you're
doing," said Alba, as she took the
ball from Frankie and threw it high
into the air.

Frankie sprinted towards it
before Kyle had even moved. He
was about to get to the ball when
he saw Kyle's foot dart out and
scuff the ground. A cloud of dirt
hit Frankie's face and he swung his
foot blindly.

"Hey, that's not fair!" yelled
Charlie.

By the time Frankie could open

his eyes, he saw Kyle running towards the goal. He'd obviously forgotten about Louise, though. Sliding across the ground, she took the ball away and left Kyle sprawling. He got to his feet, his face an angry red.

Louise kicked the ball sideways at the wall of one of the ranch buildings. It bounced off, around Neil, and right back into her path.

"Nice work, Louise!" Alba cried.

But Neil was chasing and he was quick. He lunged, grabbing Louise around the waist and pulling her to the ground.

"Foul!" shouted Charlie.

"Aussie rules!" said Neil, picking up the ball in his hands and running with it towards the goal. Frankie knew that Aussie rules football was more like rugby than soccer, but now they were about to lose. Frankie couldn't let that happen!

Neil threw the ball in front of him, ready to kick it. Nothing could stop him . . .

Max barked wildly. Enough to distract Neil. His foot skimmed off the edge of the ball. It hit the post and rebounded.

"That dog put me off," he said.

"*Doggie* rules!" barked Max.

Everyone stopped, and looked at Frankie's dog. "Did that dog just speak?" said Kyle.

"Don't be silly!" said Charlie. "You've been spending too long in the sun."

Louise managed to get the loose ball, and passed to Frankie. Kyle ran at him, diving into a rugby tackle, but Frankie took a step back and watched him fly past. Then, with another sidestep he chipped the ball into the goal.

"Frankie's team wins!" cried Alba.

Kyle picked himself up out of the dirt and dusted down his clothes. He looked so angry that Frankie backed away. But then he grinned and shook hands with Frankie. "You beat us fair and square," he said. "Two camels are yours!"

CHAPTER 6

The two camels were called
Grumpy and Lumpy, Kyle told
them as he fastened the saddles
into place. He placed a riding crop
on Grumpy's nose and whistled.
The camel buckled its front knees.
Frankie used a stepladder to
climb on in front of its hump. The

animal didn't smell particularly nice.

Alba got on behind him.

"Better put any belongings in the saddlebags," said Kyle. "You'll need your hands on the reins."

Frankie dropped his football into a saddlebag along with Alba's boomerang, then put his hat back on.

"Hey, what about me?" whispered Max. "I can't trek across the outback — my legs are only small."

Frankie leant down and picked up his dog, placing him carefully in the other saddlebag. Neil was helping Charlie and Louise on to the other camel, Lumpy.

Kyle tapped Grumpy on the flank and the animal jerked up its head, then rose to standing on wobbly legs. He gave Frankie the crop. Frankie gripped on tight to the creature's flanks with his thighs. It suddenly seemed a long way down to the ground.

Kyle pointed. "Just follow the trail," he said. "It will take you to Uluru. The camels know the route, but make sure you're back before dusk! My parents will go mad otherwise."

Frankie had ridden a horse before, and he hoped this wasn't much different. He squeezed his

heels and the camel set off at
a slow, shambling pace, Lumpy
following behind.

"I hope we can find the animals
safe," Frankie said.

"They'll probably have looked
for some shade," said Alba, her
brow furrowed. "If we search near

the mountain, we might find their footprints again."

"I can sniff them out!" said Max.

Alba gasped and Frankie froze in the saddle.

"OK, you'd better tell me what's going on," said the girl. "That was definitely your dog."

"Kangaroos have a very peculiar aroma," said Max. "Like sheep mixed with cows."

"Erm . . . " Frankie began.

"Oh, I may as well tell her myself," said Max, peeping out of the saddlebag. "His football is magic. We're not really tourists — we're from the other side of the world and we came through a portal chasing an escaped kangaroo called Madge. Simple, really."

"And you can talk?" said Alba.

"That's hardly the weirdest part, if you think about it," said Max.

"I suppose not," said Alba. "This is turning into a very strange day."

"Madge is from a safari park in Great Britain," said Frankie. "She left her baby behind, so we need to get her home as soon as we can. I'm sorry we lied to you."

"That's OK," said Alba. "I think I might have called a doctor if you'd tried to be honest up front. They'd have blamed too much sun!"

They rode the camels for ages, and the mountain grew with every mile, looming high above them and so wide it filled the horizon. Alba passed around flasks of water. It was a relief when the sun finally began to sink over the top of the mountain and the temperature dropped.

"We don't have long," said Alba. "The camels need to be back at dusk — and I don't want Dingo to be out at night time. It gets really cold."

The camel knelt down again when Frankie placed the crop on its head, and he climbed to the ground. Max leapt from the saddlebag.

"I think I can smell kangaroo!" he said, lowering his snout to the ground.

The others all dismounted too. Max paused at some prints in the ground. Frankie knelt down to inspect them. They were the same marks as earlier, to be sure, but there was no sign of a dog's paw marks too. The kangaroo trail led right towards the mountain's red rocky wall. Alba's lip trembled.

"Don't worry," said Frankie. "I'm sure Dingo won't be far away."

Frankie followed the tracks. It was only when he got close to the rock face that he saw that it wasn't solid. There were gaps, leading into darkness beyond.

"Uluru is full of caves," said Alba. "Follow me!"

She took one of the bags from the camel's saddle and looped it over her shoulder, then she gave the other, with the football and the boomerang, to Frankie.

They entered the cave mouth and the air instantly cooled. It smelled musty. Alba took out a torch and lit up the way ahead. "Dingo!" she called. Her voice echoed back.

They hadn't gone far when Frankie saw strange markings on the walls. "What's that?" he asked, pointing. Alba brought the torch's beam around. Frankie was speechless — the walls were covered in drawings! Figures and animals, and other shapes like stars and swirls, all sketched in yellow and white paints. Charlie reached up to touch them with his glove, but Alba grabbed his hand.

"These drawings are thousands of years old!" she said.

"Sorry," muttered Charlie.

"It's OK," said Alba. "Uluru is sacred. We don't even like to climb it."

They continued into the gloominess. It was hard to see

tracks anymore, but Max kept his nose pressed to the ground. "Madge definitely came this way," he said.

Suddenly the torch picked out points of light ahead, like two gleaming gold coins – eyes! Then a shadow moved and Frankie heard the panicked shuffle of steps. Alba followed with the torch beam. Then there were four eyes – two low down and two above. Frankie took a couple of seconds to work out what he was seeing. Madge had Dingo in her pouch! *She must be missing her baby,* thought Frankie.

Her nostrils flared and her head

jerked left and right. The kangaroo's powerful tail thumped the ground.

"It's OK," said Frankie, stepping forward slowly with his hands raised.

"Be careful," said Alba. "A kangaroo's legs could easily knock you out."

"And they can box too!" said Charlie. "I read it in the safari park guide."

Great! thought Frankie. Dingo was peering out of the pouch, ears pricked up. Even if they managed to open up the portal, they still needed to somehow separate the two animals.

"Dingo, come to me," said
Alba. Frankie turned and saw her
crouching down, arms outstretched.

He was only a few metres from
the kangaroo when she made a
snorting sound and leapt into
the air. Frankie staggered away
as Madge's back legs thrust like
pistons towards him. He tripped
and fell to the ground. Then he saw
Madge bound right over the top of
him, barrelling past the others and
back towards the cave entrance.

"After them!" cried Charlie.

Frankie leapt to his feet and ran
in pursuit. As they burst into the
light again, they saw that Lumpy

and Grumpy were blocking the kangaroo's exit. They whinnied while Madge hopped back and forth, looking for a way through. Dingo whined as he was thrown from the pouch, then scampered quickly back to Alba's feet. She scooped him up and he nuzzled his snout against her neck, wagging his tail.

Madge shot under Lumpy's legs, bouncing towards the open desert.

I can't let her get away again! Frankie thought. *Not when we've come this far.*

In desperation, he drew the football out of the bag he was

carrying. It might not be enough to stop her, but it would be a distraction. He took a step, tossing the ball in front of him, and kicked it hard. It arced over the kangaroo's head. Madge skidded as she watched the ball's flight.

But as it landed, the football didn't bounce.

It disappeared into the dusty ground. *Oh no!*

Frankie ran after it, as the kangaroo edged closer to where the ball had landed.

"Stop!" Louise called, but it was too late.

The kangaroo had vanished!

Frankie reached the same spot and saw a portal shrinking on the ground. By the time his friends arrived at his side, it had completely gone, leaving only red dust.

There was no sign of the magic football.

"Er . . . what now?" said Charlie. "No football means no way home."

Frankie's heart sank to his heels. His friend was right.

We're trapped here!

CHAPTER 7

Frankie hardly knew what to say. This was all his fault. The magic football had *always* been their ticket back. Without it, they were stuck thousands of miles from home.

Dingo nuzzled against his leg.

"Don't worry," said Alba. "You

can use the phone back at the camel ranch. Call your parents."

Charlie had his head in his gloves. "I think my parents might have a hard time believing me," he said.

"And mine might have a hard time paying for the air fare home!" said Louise.

Frankie thought about his mum and dad at the safari park. When they heard about this, Kevin's bad reports from school wouldn't seem so bad.

Grumpy and Lumpy were the only ones who didn't seem worried. They lowered themselves again for Frankie and his friends to clamber on.

As the camels climbed to their feet and set off, the road seemed very long.

"I suppose this is the end of our adventures," said Louise. "I'll probably be grounded until I'm eighteen."

Frankie managed a weak smile. He looked at Max, who was nestled back in the saddlebag.

"You're not saying much," he muttered.

Max cocked his head.

"I said, you're very quiet," said Frankie.

Max whined softly, and Frankie suddenly understood. "You can't

speak any more, can you?" he said.
"Because the football has gone."

Max barked and Frankie felt
sadder than ever. He'd enjoyed
being able to chat with his pet and
leaned across to stroke Max behind
the ears. "I'll find you an extra juicy
bone, when we get home."

If we get home, a little voice in
his head added.

It was dark by the time they
reached the ranch. Kyle and Neil
were waiting by the gates.

"Quick, get those camels in the
yard!" said the elder of the two.
"Mum and Dad will be back any
minute."

Frankie guided Grumpy back towards the pen, and climbed off first. He was about to go and ask to use the phone for a long-distance call when he noticed something very strange. One of the saddlebags was glowing slightly.

"Alba," he said. "What's in there?"

She saw the glow too, and drew a sharp breath. "My boomerang!" she said.

Frankie felt a flicker of hope as she took it out. The wood was shining unnaturally.

Could it be that some of the football's magic had rubbed off, while it was in the bag with the boomerang?

"May I?" Frankie asked, holding out his hand.

Alba handed Frankie the boomerang, which felt slightly warm to the touch. He looked around, to make sure Kyle and

Neil weren't watching. Louise and Charlie gathered close.

Frankie drew back his arm, and hurled the boomerang across the pen. It disappeared in the darkening sky.

"Not a great throw," said Alba. "But it was only your second attempt."

Frankie grinned. "I don't think it was ever going to come back," he said. "Follow me."

He led them away from the back of the ranch, until they came across the boomerang on the ground. Beside it, the air was shimmering like a heat haze. A portal had opened, but it was growing smaller. They didn't have much time.

"What is it?" whispered Alba.

"It's our way home," said Frankie.

"You hope," muttered Charlie.

"Only one way to find out!" said Louise.

Frankie picked up the boomerang and handed it to Alba. "Thanks for everything," he said.

Alba was still staring at the ground, clutching Dingo in one hand and her boomerang in the other. "Good luck!" she said.

Frankie closed his eyes, and stepped into the portal.

*

"Hey!" shouted a female voice.

Frankie turned dizzily and saw a park ranger jogging towards them. It was the same woman who they'd spoken to earlier. Only now she looked angry.

"I thought I told you – NO BALL GAMES!"

Frankie and his friends were all standing beside the Australian enclosure of the park. He spotted the football at his feet. He quickly used his toe to flick it into his hands.

"Sorry," he said. "I finally found it."

The ranger scowled.

Louise smiled at her. "Any luck

with that missing kangaroo?" she asked.

The ranger shook her head. "No. It's a complete mystery. We can't work out how . . ."

Charlie's hand shot up, pointing towards the enclosure. The ranger spun around and Frankie saw it too. Madge the kangaroo was standing beside the fence.

"Wh . . . what?" the ranger stammered. She pressed her radio transmitter. "Attention all rangers," she said. "Madge is here."

"*Are you sure, Gill?*" crackled a voice.

"Clear as day," said the ranger.

"I'm looking right at her! Bring her joey back to the enclosure at once."

Frankie and his friends stepped back as the male ranger came rushing up, holding the baby kangaroo. As soon as it saw its mother, it leapt out of his hands and bounded towards her, mewling in excitement. Louise giggled as it scrambled up Madge's fur and leapt head-first into her pouch. A moment later it peered out.

Frankie's parents were just getting back into their car at the head of the queue. "Come on, you lot," said Frankie's mum. "They're opening the enclosure again."

Frankie almost laughed. It felt like they'd been gone for most of the day, but time ran differently when the magic football was involved.

They all piled into the car and Max leapt into the boot.

As they drove into the enclosure, kangaroos bounded alongside the car.

"Aren't you going to take a picture?" asked Frankie's mum.

Frankie looked at the camera hanging around his neck. He suddenly thought, *Will the snaps from Uluru be on it? That will take some explaining.*

"I think the battery has died," he said.

He twisted round to stroke behind Max's ears. "Quite an adventure, hey boy?"

Max gave a bark and Frankie's mum laughed.

"It's almost as though he can understand you!" she said, as they drove off.

Frankie winked at Max. "Don't be silly," he said, turning back around in his seat. He waved to the kangaroos as they passed, and Madge lifted a paw, almost like she was waving back. "Animals aren't that clever!"

ACKNOWLEDGEMENTS

Many thanks to everyone at Hachette Children's Group; Neil Blair, Zoe King, Daniel Teweles and all at The Blair Partnership; Luella Wright for bringing my characters to life; special thanks to Michael Ford for all his wisdom and patience; and to Steve Kutner for being a great friend and for all his help and guidance, not just with the book but with everything.

Could you be a winner, like Frankie?

Take a look at the pictures in this book. Somewhere, we have hidden a miniature Australian flag, just like this one:

Can you find it?

For the chance to win an exclusive Frankie's Magic Football goodie bag, write down the page number this secret image appears on then visit **www.frankiesmagicfootball. co.uk/competitions** and ask a grown up to help you fill in the form.

Once you've completed your entry, you will be able to download a template to colour in your own Australian flag.

This competition is open to all readers. Closing date is 31.05.2015. For full terms and conditions, see the website.

Frankie wishes you all good luck. Remember, everyone has talent!

FRANKIE'S MAGIC FOOTBALL
WEBSITE

Have you had a chance to check out
frankiesmagicfootball.co.uk yet?

Get involved in **competitions**, find out **news** and
updates about the series, play **games** and watch
videos featuring the author, **Frank Lampard!**

Visit the site to join
Frankie's FC today!